This book belongs to

Jaumse Anders ✦

'To my wife Dawn – you make me real' Justin Birch
'For Mum, Dad and Ste with lots of love xxx' Helen Poole

This edition published in 2021 by Alligator Books Ltd.
Cupcake is an imprint of Alligator Books Ltd.
Gadd House, Arcadia Avenue, London N3 2JU

Written by Justin C H Birch
Illustrated by Helen Poole

Printed in China 1793

Henry's
Pirate Surprise

cupcake

Henry's Uncle Richard was a toymaker and lived above his shop. Henry loved to visit as his uncle would always surprise him with new toys. Then he would ask Henry to play with them over the weekend.

"You are my chief toy tester," his uncle would say. "It's a very important job."

This time his uncle had a special surprise for him. On a large table stood an enormous wooden ship.

"Wow, a pirate ship!" exclaimed Henry. "It's amazing!"

"This is the 'Stinking Rose', the finest pirate galleon to sail the seven seas. But this is not the surprise," said his uncle.

"Really? But it's fabulous. What could possibly be more surprising than this?" asked Henry.

"I think that honour falls to me," said a voice from inside the ship.
"The ship can talk?" Henry's mouth fell wide open.

"The ship doesn't talk," his uncle started to explain, but then a
door opened on the deck and a tiny pirate captain walked into view,
took off his hat with a flourish and bowed to Henry.
"Captain Eightpiece at your service."

Henry couldn't believe his eyes, "This is the best toy you have ever made, Uncle Richard!"

"Henry, Captain Eightpiece is real and so is the rest of his crew," Uncle Richard whispered.

"Absolutely!" cried Captain Eightpiece. "My crew and I have been looking for a good ship. Fortunately, we came to your uncle's shop and found this wonderful vessel. We sail tomorrow."

"But you can't be real, you're only six inches high!" exclaimed Henry. "Six and a half, actually." Captain Eightpiece stood tall. "Well, if I'm not real then you won't be able to feel this, will you?" He took out his cutlass, marched over to Henry and poked him in the hand. "Ouch!" shouted Henry.

"He did that to me too," smiled Henry's uncle. "Then, he paid me for the ship with gold coins. We're going to help Captain Eightpiece and his crew launch the ship tomorrow."

"Let me introduce you to my crew, dear boy," said the captain. "Men! On deck now!" he roared and four tiny men appeared on the deck of the ship.

"This is Barney Call, the mate.
He is second in command to me."

"And Limpey Pit, the bosun. He
makes sure all the crew do
their jobs properly."

"Perry Winkle is the second mate and is in charge of navigation."

"And finally, Razor Clam, the helmsman. He mans the helm, which means he steers the ship."

Captain Eightpiece looked up at Henry. "We could do with a cabin boy, but unfortunately you're a bit . . . well, big. However, we've got lots of jobs to do. If you want to help that'd be nice?"

So Henry scrubbed the deck with a toothbrush.

He stacked marbles that could be used to fire in the cannon.

He put the pirate flag on the top of the mast.

And he filled matchboxes with flour, cereal and other foods ready for the long journey.

Henry stayed with the pirate crew until bedtime. The crew told him about their adventures sailing the high seas, battling scary monsters and finding treasure. He could have listened to them all night.

When Uncle Richard told him it was time for bed, Henry reluctantly bid the pirates good night and promised to help them launch the Stinking Rose in the river in the morning. Then he went up to bed and was asleep in minutes.

A noise downstairs woke Henry in the middle of the night.
He heard a door squeak and then the sound of muffled voices.

Somebody was breaking into the toyshop!

Henry's
bed

Henry crept out of bed and tiptoed out of his room
and across the corridor to his uncle's room.

Then a voice from downstairs drifted up to Henry.

"Blimey Dave, look at that pirate ship. That'd fetch a pretty penny. Let's just nick that and get out of here smartish."

Henry knew he needed to scare the burglars away. He was desperately trying to think of a plan when he felt something run up his pyjama trouser leg, along his arm and then he heard a voice whisper in his ear . . .

"Trying to figure out how to catch the burglars are you? Good man." Captain Eightpiece swung from Henry's ear onto his nose and looked him in the eyes. "Limpey, Barney and Perry are hiding in the ship, ready to surprise them. Razor's underneath the table, up to no good I'd imagine."

"What's your plan?" whispered Henry.
"We're pirates my boy! We'll repel them!" And with that, Captain Eightpiece jumped off Henry's nose, ran down his arm and onto the floor where he disappeared into the darkness.

The two burglars were now struggling with the Stinking Rose.
"Help me lift this ship up," wheezed the shorter one.
The larger thief bent over the ship, "Ouch! Something bit my hand!"
"Shhh, you big baby," the smaller burglar scoffed, "put your back
into it. Ow, something bit me too. Ouch. And again!"

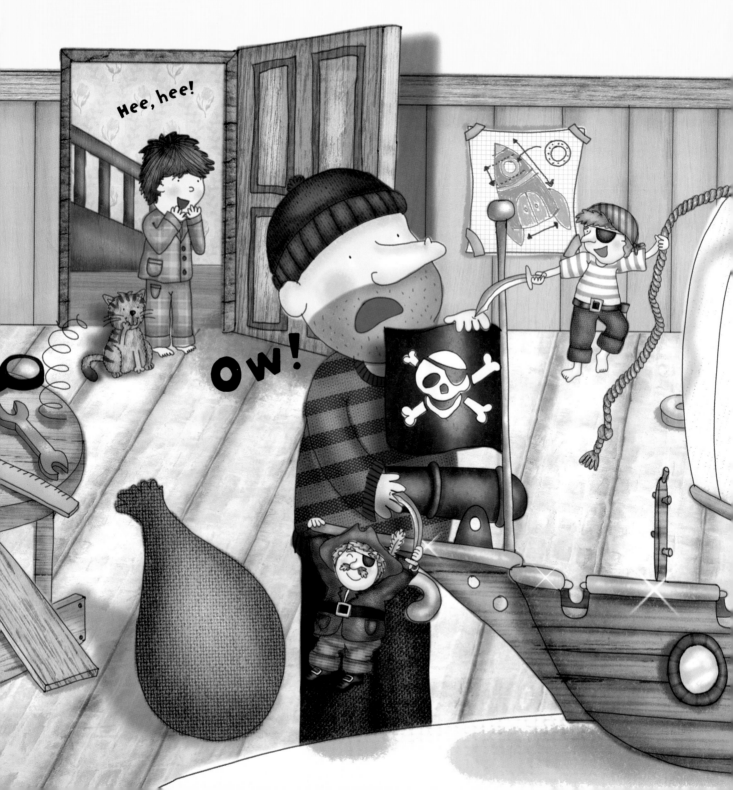

Henry tried not to laugh. The crew were poking the burglars' hands with swords. Then, Henry heard the buzzing of an engine. He looked up and saw a remote control helicopter. Captain Eightpiece was throwing tiny bags of flour into the thieves eyes! "Stop, you scoundrels!" Captain Eightpiece shouted.

"Quick, run! Let's get out of here," cried the thieves.

But when the burglars tried to run they tripped over. Razor had tied their shoelaces together!

"Yahoo! Henry wake your uncle and call the police," called Captain Eightpiece jumping onto the larger burglar. Razor jumped onto the shorter one's chin and threatened him with his cutlass.

Thump!

"Stone me, I'm seeing things. There are pirate pixies in here," croaked the big thief as he fainted.

Henry's uncle had already called the police when Henry went to get him. He and Henry went downstairs to find the two moaning burglars tied up, but there was no sign of the pirates. Only if you listened very carefully could you hear laughter coming from the *Stinking Rose*.

The police arrived and took the burglars away. They congratulated Henry and his uncle for catching the two men and told them that there would be a reward. The police asked if they knew why the burglars kept talking about six-inch high pirates, but Henry and Uncle Richard pretended not to know.

The next morning Henry and Uncle Richard carried the Stinking Rose to
the river and helped Captain Eightpiece launch the ship.
It floated perfectly.
Captain Eightpiece thanked Henry and Uncle Richard for the ship.

"Good spot of fun last night, Henry. If you ever grow smaller you can definitely be my cabin boy!" And with a flourish of his hat and a graceful bow, Captain Eightpiece jumped onto the Stinking Rose and he and his crew sailed off towards the seven seas and new adventures.

The End!